FRANK BANGED A FEMALE BIGFOOT

© 2018

DADDYDRUMMER Publishing and Productions

All rights reserved.

WINNER

Best Reads Of
2018

Frank Banged a
Female Bigfoot

2018 Unexplained Writings Awards ©

From the Author -

I know what you are thinking. Did I read this title correctly? Does it actually say "Frank banged a female Bigfoot"? Yes, yes it does. This is the story that recounts the events leading up to, during and after the time that Frank spent Fucking a female Bigfoot. The story focuses on three unlikely friends, Conspiracy Theories, Fake News, Government cover ups and WTF moments.

There will be doubters, there will be skeptics and there will be finger pointers but I can assure you that Frank did indeed did have a sexual encounter with a female Bigfoot. So please read this story with an open mind and save your conclusions until the last page when you will have to decide if you are on team Frank or team Conspiracy Theory.

I decided to write this in format similar to a screenplay to allow the reader to feel fully involved in every scene and understand the emotions of all involved.

If you believe in Bigfoot, great. If you do not, then maybe you will change your mind after reading this. Either way, enjoy the read.

This book is dedicated to *Jennifer*. You helped breathe life into Quoteboy.

"Smell my fingers"

- *Frank 2018*

CHAPTER ONE - ITS IN THE PREP WORK

Day. Exterior. Woods.

Bill, Frank and Quoteboy are hiking through Thompson Creek woods in Claremont California. An area long thought to be haunted and filled with decades of folk lore and the infamous bleeding trees. This is a typical weekend hike for Bill. This is Frank's first time hiking in his life. Bill and Frank are both in their mid- twenties. Bill is fit and healthy and Frank is overweight and unhealthily. Bill is dressed in a tan tank top and green cargo pants with combat style leather boots with a waterproof backpack hanging over his left shoulder while Frank is wearing an oversized white Tupac T-shirt covered in fresh sweat stains with baggy blue and purple stripped 1980's Muscle pants and tattered red Chuck Taylor Converse sneakers and an overstuffed white pillow case hanging over his shoulder. Quoteboy is a thirty-nine-year-old skinny Conspiracy Theorist germaphobe Republican who constantly uses air quotes as he speaks, usually emphasizing the wrong words. Quoteboy is dressed in state of the art hiking gear and an oversized backpack and a Make America Great Again hat. Frank is huffing and puffing and reaches to grab onto a tree for support as he calls out to Bill who is several yards ahead of him. Quoteboy stops next to Frank and takes out a digital thermometer scanner and scans Frank's body temperature.

Frank

Yo dude, hold up. I need to catch my breath.

Frank pushes Quoteboy's thermometer away from his body as Bill turns around and hesitantly walks back towards Frank.

Bill

Look at you. Your covered in sweat and sound like you're having a stroke.

Quoteboy begins to use his air quotes as he speaks.

Quoteboy

Frank's internal "body" temperature is 99.1.

Bill

So? Its hot out and he is fat.

Quoteboy

"Point" taken.

Frank takes his hand off of the tree and realizes it is covered in a sticky substance. He raises his hand to his face.

Frank

What the Fuck is this?

Bill

That's a Bleeding Tree, well its actually just a Spruce tree with a fungal infection but calling it a Bleeding Tree just sounds so much better. Idiots come out here to these woods just to see these Bleeding Trees, like they are some weird spiritual thing.

Frank tries to wipe the wet tree gew off of his hand onto his shirt. In doing so it looks like the giant lithograph head of Tupac is bleeding.

Frank

And it's just a tree with a fungal infection?

Bill

That's it. So are you and Tupac ready? We have a lot of ground to cover. We want to keep moving to keep our heart rates up and really get in a good workout.

Quoteboy

We should keep "an" eye on your internal body temperature. Liberals tend to run hot from "all" their Political Correctness.

Frank and Bill look at Quoteboy with glaring expressions.

Frank

Hold up. I need a snack.

Frank lowers his pillow case and digs through it, removing items and placing them on the ground until he finds what he is looking for. He removes multiple Snickers candy bars, a bag of mini donuts, a stick of Land O Lakes butter and two bags of potato chips until he pulls out a half of a Subway sub. He unwraps it and begins to eat it as Bill just stares at him shaking his head from side to side.

Bill

Seriously?

Frank takes a huge bite of his sub sandwich.

Frank

What?

Bill points at Frank.

Bill

Look at you, you're not dressed to be out here, you look like your dressed to be hitting a bong on the couch at your brother's house. And is that a Fucking Big Daddy Kane pillow case?

Frank

I couldn't find my backpack. This is fine it has all the essentials for the woods.

Bill

Like a half-eaten Subway sub?

Frank takes a huge bite of his sub sandwich.

Frank

Protein Bill. I need protein if I am going to be hiking.

Bill

OK. Protein is good but what about the chips, donuts and a butter stick. Who the Fuck eats butter sticks?

Frank

It's a condiment for my chips. You know like ketchup for French fries.

Bill

Butter is not a condiment. It's a fat.

Quoteboy applies hand sanitizer to his fingers.

Quoteboy

I think you "are" both overlooking the bacteria factor here. That sandwich containing cold cut meats was not refrigerated and kept "in" an environment that breeds bacteria growth. Most notably Salmonella which comes across our open borders with "all the" undocumented immigrants who arrive to take our jobs.

Bill glares at Quoteboy.

Bill

Bacteria won't kill Frank. I once watched Frank drink a seven-day old family sized container of KFC gravy. It was chunky with green blobs floating in it. Nothing happened. Remember that Frank?

Frank

I do. Quoteboy, trust me, bacteria aint' got Shit on me. And you Bill, why do you have to judge? You always judge me and my decisions.

Bill

Being out here, is all in the prep work. I told you last week what you needed to wear and bring with you to these woods and you didn't do one thing I said.

Frank

Not true. I got that fire starter thing you told me to get. I was at Harbor Freight. I used a 20% off coupon.

Frank rummages through his pillow case and pulls out a fire starter and shows it to Bill.

Bill

Great, at least you can heat up your butter condiment if needed.

Frank

Just cuz your dressed like Lewis from Deliverance doesn't mean you're more prepared than me. Your muscles have muscles. How does that even happen?

Bill

I treat my body like a temple. You on the other hand choose to treat yours like an amusement park.

Frank takes a huge bite of his Subway sub.

Frank

Damn now I want cotton candy. Why did you have to go and say amusement park?

Bill

Look at Quoteboy. He's dressed like he just popped off the pages of an L.L Bean catalog. He's prepped and ready to go. Minus the Trump hat. So let's go. Eat your protein as you walk, we are losing daylight.

Frank jams the rest of the Subway sub into his mouth.

Frank

I'm done.

Bill

You just ate a six-inch sub in four bites?

Frank

What?

Quoteboy

That does not "help" with proper digestion. I'm just saying.

Frank

I don't digest, I just chew, swallow and Shit.

Quoteboy looks at Frank with a bewildered expression on his face.

Quoteboy.

You know more "people" attended Trump's Presidential inauguration than are physically on this Earth.

Bill laughs as Frank just shakes his head.

Frank

That makes absolutely no sense.

Quoteboy

Typical response "from" a Liberal who can't see that our Financial infrastructure is about to collapse "and" Marshall Law will be declared.

Frank

Do you think before you spit out these lies and conspiracy theory Bull Shit?

Quoteboy

That was an Alternative Fact of Trath.

Frank

Trath? You mean Truth. Alternative Fact of Truth.

Quoteboy

No I mean Trath. Trath is "the" new Truth of "the" Conservative Movement. A Trath is the alternative way of creatively saying a "semi-lie" to further one's agenda "but" not actually lying per the proper definition of the word. Thus, I mean Trath.

Frank

It's not a word.

Quoteboy

Yes "it" is.

Frank

No it is not.

Quoteboy

"Yes it" is.

Frank

Fuck it. I give up.

Bill laughs.

Bill

I knew you would blink on that.

Frank points at Bill and then at Quoteboy.

Frank

Fuck you and Fuck you Quoteboy and stop Fucking air quoting with your fingers it is so God Damn annoying!

Bill turns away and continues on the path followed closely by Quoteboy as Frank collects his pillow case and tries to quickly follow. Frank hears breaking branches behind him so he stops and turns around. He looks off into the woods but doesn't see anything. Bill realizes Frank is not moving so he turns around and yells to Frank. Quoteboy stops as well.

Bill

Frank, what the Fuck are you doing?

Frank

I thought I heard something.

Bill

Like what?

Frank

I don't know. Branches breaking maybe. I'm not sure.

Bill

The woods are silent until they're not?

Frank

Ok Henry David Thoreau. What the Fuck does that even mean?

Bill

It means there are noises all around you out here. The woods will let you know when it wants to be heard? A birds call, a falling branch, noises happen out here.

Frank

Great, my creep factor just shot through the Fucking roof. Wait up.

Frank turns back towards Bill and continues down the tree lined path. He hurries to catch up to Bill and Quoteboy. Frank is visibly out of breath and struggling to keep up.

Bill

Look Frank, I think it's great you want to try and lose some weight and get healthier by joining Quoteboy and me on this hike. I can see this isn't easy for you.

Frank wipes the sweat that is dripping down his face with his left hand.

Frank

I'm fine.

Quoteboy *stops next to Frank and takes out a digital thermometer scanner and scans Frank's body temperature. Frank swats away Quoteboy's arm.*

Quoteboy

99.3. He is "going" to boil soon.

Bill

Quoteboy might be on to something here. You are looking worse. You look like you just had four mini heart attacks in past ten yards.

Frank

I'm fine.

Bill

Your fine? Your face is currently a shade of purple not known to any color charts.

The sound of moving branches can be heard behind them. They both pause and turn around and look.

Frank

That's what I heard before.

Bill

It's nothing.

Frank

Yeh sure. It's probably some Michael Myers type killer stalking the Fuck out of us.

Bill unsnaps the flap to his knife holster and pulls out his knife to show Frank.

Bill

Being out here, is all in the prep work. I am prepared.

Frank

Good to know Rambo.

Quoteboy

It is more plausible that it is an Elite Hitman team "for" the Democratic National Party to distract from Hilary "and" Bengasi.

Bill and Frank both shake their heads at Quoteboy.

Bill

Seriously?

Quoteboy applies hand sanitizer to his fingers.

Quoteboy

What? Don't you "both listen" to Alex Jones?

Frank

I'm all for questioning the government and society and Shit but you take it just too far Quoteboy.

Bill

Neither of us listen to that Shit. I would rather put my Dick in a vise than listen to that Shit.

Frank

I wouldn't do that. You know, put your Dick in a vice. Speaking from experience it hurts like a Mutha Fucka.

Quoteboy begins to speak but is cutoff by Bill in mid-sentence.

Quoteboy

But "Alex" says juice boxes turn people Gay.

Bill

Shut the Fuck up Quoteboy. Come on let's keep moving. We are losing daylight.

Bill turns back towards the path and continues on his way as Frank follows him slowly as he is sweating and tired.

Frank

Losing daylight? We haven't even eaten dinner yet. No seriously I'm hungry. Can we stop for a meal? Maybe even just pick some fruits and berries and other healthy shit.

Quoteboy

I brought "some homemade" IV bags of Glucose if we need them.

Bill and Frank both shake their heads at Quoteboy.

Quoteboy (continued)

Glucose is "essential" to the human body.

Frank

Dude you have some real issues.

Quoteboy looks at Frank with a confused expression on his face as he applies hand sanitizer to his fingers.

Quoteboy

I don't follow "you Frank." Are you just upset that Trump has created more new jobs since taking office "than' every other President in the world combined since the dawn of time? The unemployment rate under Trump is negative 100%. Alex "says" Trump created two jobs for "every" American in the country. That is a Trath.

Frank

I'm hot, sweaty and you are pissing me off severely with your Trath's.

Quoteboy

You are a "Bernie" lover.

Bill yells back at Frank and Quoteboy.

Bill (yelling)

Come on let's go!

Frank

I would but Mike Pence junior here won't shut the Fuck up.

Frank points at Quoteboy.

Frank(continued)

Your President is orange.

Quoteboy rubs hand sanitizer on his fingers.

Quoteboy

Oranges "have" Vitamin C.

Frank points at Quoteboy as Quoteboy sticks out his tongue.

Frank

Enough with the Fucking air quotes. Seriously don't your arms ever get tried?

Quoteboy

Alex Jones "has" made 287 predictions since 1999 and 3 of "those" predictions have come true.

Frank

That has nothing to do with what I just asked you and listen to what you said. His batting average for predictions sucks.

Quoteboy

Typical Liberal "focusing" on the negative.

Frank points at Quoteboy's hat as he walks away from him.

Frank

Your President is still Orange.

Bill yells back at Frank and Quoteboy.

Bill (yelling)

Come on let's go!

CHAPTER TWO - FOLK LORE AND TWINKIES

Night. Exterior. Woods.

Frank, Quoteboy and Bill are sitting around a camp fire. Bill and Quoteboy are eating protein bars while Frank is eating a box of Twinkies. Bill is staring at Frank, shaking his head from side to side.

Frank

What? I'm hungry. I need some sugar.

Bill

Who brings a box of Twinkies on a hike? How many are in that box? How many?

Frank is talking with his mouth full of Twinkies.

Frank

It's a 24 pack.

Bill

A 24 pack? You bought that new for this hike?

Frank

Yes.

Bill

And how many are left?

Frank looks into the box and then looks back up at Bill.

Frank

It looks like four.

Bill

Looks like four? So you have eaten twenty Twinkies since we started this hike?

Quoteboy

"Wow."

Frank

Maybe. I think one might have fallen out.

Bill

This is an overnight hike. One day. Nobody needs to bring a 24 pack of Twinkies for an overnight hike. And where do you get a huge ass 24 pack of Twinkies?

Frank

Costco.

Bill stokes the fire.

Bill

It's not normal to eat 20 Twinkies.

Frank slouches his body down.

Frank

Nineteen, I told you one fell out and I am out of my element. I eat when I am nervous.

Bill

What is there to be nervous about?

Frank

Oh I don't know, maybe murderers stalking us in the woods, maybe a Fucking big ass bear, hell maybe even Bigfoot is out there.

Quoteboy

Don't forget "the" Elite Squad of Democratic Hitmen.

Bill

Quoteboy shut the Fuck up. Frank why do you worry so much?

Frank

I just do.

Bill stokes the fire some more as Quoteboy takes out his digital thermometer scanner and scans the campfire.

Bill

It's the wrong time of year for Bears, it's too much work for murderers to stalk this deep in the woods, there is no Elite Democratic Hitman Squad and Bigfoot isn't real.

Frank sits upright and points at Bill.

Frank

Bigfoot's real.

Bill lets out a laugh as he stokes the fire with a stick.

Quoteboy

I agree with Frank. "There are" statistically far too many sightings for Bigfoot not to be real. The late great Art "Bell" believes this.

Bill

Sure. Whatever.

Frank

There is plenty of evidence out there. Plenty.

Bill

Grainy blurry videos and dark still photos. Absolutely no bones, no hair samples. Yeh, that's evidence. Its folk lore and nothing more.

Frank

What about the Patterson film footage? Undeniable evidence. If you watch the walk, the gate, it is not human, thus it is a Bigfoot.

Quoteboy

The Patterson "footage" was altered by multiple Democratic Senators in the summer of 1975 in anticipation of the rigged 2016 Democratic Primary where Hilary came out victorious. Thus making it null "and" void.

Bill and Frank just shake their heads at Quoteboy.

Bill

Sorry guys. I just don't believe in Bigfoot.

Frank

You can't possibly deny the Patterson film footage?

Bill

Watch me.

Quoteboy

Bad choice Frank. Altered footage, Democratic "cover" up, making it null and void. A better film choice would be the Carson film footage of 2001 where a Bigfoot was seen near ground zero of the World Trade Center carrying C-4 explosives. Ask Alex Jones.

Frank and Bill just glare at Quoteboy and shake their heads from side to side.

Frank

Quoteboy shut the Fuck up. Bill, you talk about prep work. I did my research. I did prep work. Did you know there were multiple Bigfoot sightings in these woods over the past fifteen years? The chances of us seeing a Bigfoot are pretty damn good.

Bill

You didn't come out here to lose weight and get healthy did you? You came out here to see Bigfoot.

Frank

No. I'm all about getting healthy this weekend. Calorie counting, sweating and stuff.

Bill stokes the fire.

Bill

By gobbling down a 24 pack of Twinkies?

Frank

I told you, one fell out.

Quoteboy applies hand sanitizer to his fingers.

Quoteboy

Do you know what is in your beloved Twinkies? Tiny micro computers are placed in the cream filling by rouge Democrats to create false exit polls during Gubernatorial Primary season which in "turn prove" that mass shootings are staged by Crisis Actors looking to disgrace the NRA and the NHL. Now that is a Trath for you. Just "ask" Hannity.

Bill looks at Quoteboy and shakes his head.

Bill

All I can say to that is what the Fuck?

Bill pulls out a sleeping bag from his backpack and places it on the ground. He unties the elastic straps and spreads out his sleeping bag with military precision. Quoteboy pulls out a small inflatable X-Files themed air mattress that inflates with the pull of a string and is covered with an Infowars novelty bed sheet.

Bill

Get a good night sleep. We are getting up at 4:30am.

Quoteboy jumps down onto his mattress.

Quoteboy

"I wish everyone" Fake News dreams.

Frank looks to his left and then to his right and then looks down at Bill's sleeping bag and Quoteboy's mattress.

Frank

Where is my sleeping bag?

Bill

It was on the prep list I gave you. You chose to bring a Village sized box of Twinkies instead.

Quoteboy

It was on the prep list. "Bill" emailed it to the both of us eleven days ago. I specifically remember this because I was online at the time "watching slow motion video" of Hilary coughing uncontrollably during her now infamous campaign run for President of the United States. Alex had multiple Alternate

Facts experts "conclude" she was dying of a deadly disease. It's a Trath.

Bill

Again all I can say is what the Fuck?

Frank

Where do I sleep? On the ground? Seriously I can't sleep in the dirt like an animal. The bugs will get me. I don't like bugs. Sleeping on the ground is what they did in the old days.

Bill throws another log onto the fire and then gets into his sleeping bag in one quick motion.

Bill

Looks like you and Tupac will be kicking it old school tonight.

Quoteboy applies hand sanitizer to his fingers.

Quoteboy

Some say that Democratic Dark State Operatives killed Tupac under "the" direction of the FBI funneled through a dummy "tax" corporation that colluded with the Russian Government in 1995.

Bill and Frank shake their heads at Quoteboy and speak at the same time.

Frank & Bill

Shut the Fuck up.

Quoetboy

The truth is "out" there boys. You just need to take the liberal blinders off "of" your eyes.

Bill

Maybe tomorrow. Right now I am closing my damn eyes. Goodnight.

Frank

No problem. I will just sleep in the dirt with the Fucking ants.

Quoteboy

You know fire ants were brought to this country by "the Democrats to" throw the

Republican Primaries and raise home heating fuel costs. It's an Alternative Fact of Trath.

Bill and Frank shake their heads at Quoteboy and speak at the same time.

Frank & Bill

Shut the Fuck up.

Quoteboy begins chanting out loud and fist pumping the sky as he Air Quotes at the same time.

Quoteboy

Lock her up. "Lock" her up. Lock 'her" up.

Bill

That isn't even relevant to what the Fuck you were talking about.

Quoteboy

Sure give Hilary a pass. Typical "for" you Bernie lovers who think Global Warming is an actual thing.

Bill

Listen, this is supposed to be a relaxing weekend and you are turning into some Political Conspiracy Bull Shit getaway.

Bill points to Quoteboy's stuffed doll.

Bill(continued)

What the Fuck is that?

Quoteboy

"Is" what?

Bill

That doll. What the Fuck is that?

Quoteboy holds up his stuffed doll with pride.

Quoteboy

This is my Attorney General Jeff Sessions doll. I sleep with "him" every night.

Bill

I give up.

CHAPTER THREE - WORST SMELLING PUSSY EVER

Night. Exterior. Campfire.

Bill is fast asleep next to the fire wrapped up in his sleeping bag when he awakens to the sounds of moans and grunts. He opens his sleepy eyes and sees something large on top of Frank. He wipes his eyes and sits up in his sleeping bag and then refocuses on what he sees. At first glance it looks like a large hairy woman sitting on Frank's belly. He refocuses again and realizes Frank is having sex with what appears to be a Bigfoot. The Bigfoot is riding Frank, gyrating back and forth and up and down. Letting out weird yelps as Frank is moaning. The Bigfoot begins to gyrate faster and yelp louder as Frank's belly flops around. The gyrations of the Bigfoot get so fast and loud and then it tilts its head back and lets out a very loud screeching sound.

The Bigfoot then gets off of Frank and walks away into the woods looking back at Bill. Frank sits upright and out of breath. Quoteboy slept through the entire encounter.

Frank

Dude tell me you saw that?

Bill points to Frank.

Bill

What the Fuck was that?

Frank

At first I thought I was dreaming and then I realized nope, I was actually Fucking a Bigfoot.

Bill gets out of his sleeping bag and reaches for his knife as he stands up visibly shaken. Bill frantically looks around the campsite into the adjoining tree line.

Bill

That's not possible.

Frank smiles wide with pride as he struggles to get up and pull up his tightie whities.

Frank

Dude I banged Bigfoot. A female Bigfoot, let me be clear. I'm not a gay Bigfooter. Not that there is anything wrong with that, I mean if your gay, I guess you'd want a gay Bigfoot to fuck you. But me, Frank banged a female Bigfoot! Quoteboy wake the Fuck up.

Frank kicks Quoteboy's air mattress and Quoteboy doesn't move and continues to snore and hug his blanket.

Bill

This is some prank of some kind right? Who put you up to this? Was that Craig in Gorilla costume?

Frank kicks Quoteboy's air mattress again. Quoteboy doesn't move.

Frank

Look at my Dick dude, still hard, still full of Bigfoot stank. Look at it!

Bill puts his hand up to shield his eyes.

Bill

I'm good thanks.

Frank brings his fingers to his face and smells them.

Frank

Wow, that is the worst smelling Pussy ever. Seriously, it's a cross between moldy cheese and old lady clothes.

Bill

OK if that wasn't a prank then tell me that was like some ugly hairy chick you met by the lake or something?

Frank adjusts his Dick in his underwear as he walks towards Bill.

Frank

Bill, I just banged a female Bigfoot. You saw it, I lived it and now we both smell it. Damn I didn't use a condom. I should have used a condom but the thing just came out of nowhere and begin to ride my cock like an amusement park ride. It was Fucking awesome! Fuck! I said amusement park. Now I want cotton candy again.

Bill

Tell me exactly what you remember.

Frank

Well you fell asleep in your sleeping bag and I was roughing it in the dirt but eventually fell asleep. I remember having a dream about Fucking a female Bigfoot and then I opened my eyes and there she was, a female Bigfoot riding my cock. Her Pussy was huge. I'm talking like really old porn star huge. I need to replenish. I burned like a million calories banging that Pussy.

Frank reaches into his pillow case and pulls out a bag of Fritos. He opens the bag and begins to eat.

Bill

Focus Frank. Focus. That's it? That's all you remember?

Frank smiles and gets excited as he talks with a mouthful of Fritos.

Frank

My baby batter is all up in that Bigfoot. Oh dude it would be so cool if we could make a hybrid Human-Bigfoot baby! I would call it Wally.

Bill begins to walk the perimeter of the camp.

Bill

It wasn't Bigfoot.

Frank

What do you mean it wasn't Bigfoot? You watched me bang that female Bigfoot. I was all up in her fur, or hair, whatever covers their bodies.

Bill

No I watched some hairy Backwoods Bitch ride your Twinkie Dick. You were not banging anything. She was doing all the work.

Frank

Wow somebody is jealous of my Bigfoot sex.

Bill

It wasn't Bigfoot.

Frank raises his fingers up towards Bill's face and sarcastically replies.

Frank

 Bigfoot sex.

Bill

For the last time, there is no such thing as Bigfoot.

Frank

I'm sorry, did you want to sniff my fingers for the worst smelling Pussy ever? This Pussy stank on my fingers is not Human, it's a Fucking Bigfoot. Now its mixed with Frito smell but it still reeks. Oh my God I want to do that again it was Fucking awesome!

Bill

It was some hairy Backwoods Meth Head.

Frank raises his fingers closer towards Bill's face as Bill knocks them away.

Frank

I'm sorry Bill but listen to yourself. We are in the middle of the woods and your saying some hairy Backwoods girl just walked into our camp and started to Fuck me. Look at me. No girl wants to Fuck me. We both know that. I haven't been laid since 2001 and that just because Beth Higgens was nervous about 9/11 and thought the world was ending.

Bill looks up at Frank and has an epiphany.

Bill

Your right. Absolutely no Human Female wants to Fuck you. None. Absolutely none. Not blind girls or deaf girls or armless girls. Nobody. Holey Shit you just Fucked a Bigfoot. Beth Higgins, after 9/11 didn't she move to Washington to become a Congressional Aid?

Frank crumbles up his Fritos bag and tosses it into the fire.

Frank

Thanks for the vote of confidence in my lady skills department. And Beth, yeh she became some Democratic Aid or some Shit like that.

Bill calms down a bit and laughs.

Bill

Maybe She works for the Democratic Hitman Squad now.

Frank laughs.

Frank

Haha yeh, I am sure Quoteboy would love that. So, what do we do now?

Bill stands up and places his knife back into its holster.

Bill

It's almost daylight. We track it. That's what we do. We are going to find that Bigfoot.

Frank raises his fingers closer towards Bill's face.

Frank

Seriously smell this. Worst smelling Pussy ever!

Bill

So you have said. Over and over again. I get it. Your fingers smell like moldy cheese and old lady clothes. You do not need to tell me another time. Am I Fucking clear.

Frank lowers his fingers but then smiles and quickly raises them again.

Frank

Seriously smell this. Worst smelling Pussy ever!

Quoteboy wakes up and rubs his eyes. He sits up and sniffs the air.

Quoteboy

Why "do I smell" moldy cheese?

Bill

It's a long story.

Frank smiles.

Frank

It is an awesome story.

Frank stares at Quoteboy's doll.

Frank(continued)

Can you put your Jeff Sessions doll away? It really creeps me the Fuck out.

Quoteboy stares at Frank in his underwear as he tucks in his Jeff Sessions doll.

Quoteboy

Why are you "not wearing" pajama's and is that a partial erection?

Frank smiles and looks down at his partial erection with pride.

Frank

Fuck yes it is.

Quoteboy

So "what" happened?

Bill

It looks like Frank banged a female Bigfoot.

Frank smiles as Quoteboy's jaw drops.

Quoteboy

The bacteria involved 'in that is" statistically off the charts.

Frank and Bill fill Quoteboy in on what just happened.

CHAPTER FOUR - BRUCE WILLIS

Day. Interior. Woods.

Bill, Quoteboy and Frank are walking through the woods following a path when they come upon some footprints. Bill kneels down to get a better look.

Frank.

Those are her footprints aren't they? Those are Bigfoot prints.

Bill

Not unless your hairy girlfriend is wearing hiking boots. These are shoe prints.

Quoteboy

Looks like the "tread" design of standard issue Democratic Hitman combat boots if you ask me.

Bill stands back up and glares at Quoteboy and then he looks around.

Frank.

Fucking quiet out here.

Bill

Too quiet.

Quoteboy rubs hand sanitizer all over his fingers and then adjusts his hat.

Quoteboy

Democratic "Hitman" quiet.

Bill glares at Quoteboy.

Frank.

Too quiet? What does that even mean? It sounds like a line from a Bruce Willis movie.

Frank tries to impersonate Bruce Willis

Frank (continued)

Everything is too quiet in these woods. Yippie Ki Yay Mutha Fucka.

Bill

I like Bruce Willis.

Frank

Hey me too. Die Hard is one of the top ten movies of all time.

Quoteboy

Who "is this" Bruce Willis?

Bill and Frank glare at Quoteboy with disbelief.

Bill

You are Fucking with us right?

Quoteboy

No. I know not of this Mr. "Willis" person.

Frank

Bruce Willis, greatest actor ever. Die Hard, Die Hard 2, 3 and a bunch of other movies nobody remembers the names to.

Quoteboy

None of what you speak of rings any bells. It must be fake news "propagated by" Hollywood elitists.

Frank reaches for a tree branch and grabs an old birds nest and throws it at Quoteboy.

Frank

You seriously have issues. Like deep, deep issues.

Bill

I find it really Fucked up you have never heard of Bruce Willis. You want to believe your conspiracy Shit, that right there is a conspiracy.

Frank

 But seriously what does too quiet mean?

Bill

I told you before. There are noises all around you out here. The woods will let you know when it wants to be heard? A birds call, a falling branch, noises happen out here. Right now it's too quiet. When you hear absolutely nothing, something is out there.

Frank reaches into his pillow case and frantically searches for something.

Frank

Did you take my Butter stick?

Bill

What?

Frank

Did you take my Fucking Butter stick? It is not in my pillow case.

Bill

Did you just seriously ask me if I took your Butter stick? No Frank, I have had no Butter cravings lately.

Frank

Well it's not here. Did you take it
Quoteboy?

Quoteboy

Why would I take it? I "cannot" digest
Animal based Fat products.

Bill

You probably dropped it somewhere. I'm
sure you have a plan B in that pillow case.

Frank reaches back into his pillow case and
*pulls out a Snickers candy bar. Bill glares at
Frank shaking his head side to side.*

Frank

What? I told you I eat when I'm nervous
and you just creeped me the Fuck out with
your I Know What You Did Last Summer
thought process about the noises and the
woods and Shit.

Bill

Come on let's keep moving.

Frank

Look I'm all for finding the Bigfoot but this was supposed to just be an overnight hike and boom back to the air conditioned F-150. How much longer are we going to be out here?

Bill

A while.

Frank

So a while being ten minutes or ten hours?

Bill stops walking and turns to face Frank.

Bill

I don't know. Why?

Frank

I'm sort of down to my last few candy bars.

Bill

Your trick or treat bag is getting low? Too bad. Let's keep moving.

Quoteboy rubs hand sanitizer on his fingers.

Quoteboy

I can give you one "of" my Glucose IV bags.

Frank

Not that desperate yet.

Quoteboy

You know who is desperate? The Democrats. "The Trump" agenda is uniting the country with all its Traths. Just ask Fox News.

Bill and Frank speak at the same time.

Bill & Frank

Shut the Fuck up.

They continue to move through the woods again. Frank is bringing up the rear covered in sweat.

Frank

How many girls have you Fucked?

Bill

Seventy-six.

Frank

Seriously?

Bill

Seriously.

Frank

Well you beat me there. I've been with two girls.

Bill

You've been with one girl, Beth Higgins. Fucking your cousin Lisa when she was passed out on the lawn after your Brother's graduation party doesn't count.

Frank

Hey Lisa wasn't passed out. For your information she was meditating and she's only my cousin by blood! And I have one on you, I have Fucked a Bigfoot. Yeh, Mr. I bang all the Bitches. Well you didn't bang this hairy Bitch. I did! Me, Frank!

Bill

You might not want to tell that to everyone. Keep it to yourself.

Frank raises his fingers up towards Bill's face and sarcastically replies.

Frank

 Bigfoot sex.

Quoteboy rubs hand sanitizer on his fingers.

Quoteboy

I have sexed "eleven" females. Ten Republican and one Independent.

Bill and Frank glare at Quoteboy with disbelief and both begin to laugh as Quoteboy rubs hand sanitizer on his fingers.

Quoteboy (continued)

Why are you "producing" laughter with your faces?

Bill and Frank try to stop laughing and keep walking.

Frank

That Quoteboy, was Fake News produced by the Dark State.

Bill and Frank continue to laugh.

Bill

You really need to learn what humor is. Let's just keep moving.

Quoteboy

Laugh all you want. Hahaha. You will not be laughing when "you realize the over" the counter Vitamin B you have been purchasing from your local chain pharmacy store is actually full of microchips. That's right the Democrats "have put" microchips into your Vitamin B supplements to track your online purchases. The only way around this is to buy pure Vitamin B supplements at a substantial markup "cost from" the Alex Jones Info Wars web site.

Frank

You seriously need to relax. Not everything is a conspiracy.

Quoteboy

"Yes" it is.

Frank

No it's not.

Quoteboy

"Yes" it is.

Frank

No it's not.

Quoteboy

"Yes" it is.

Frank

I give the Fuck up.

Bill begins to laugh.

Bill

I knew you would blink on that one.

They continue to walk for several miles until they come upon a wood and stone decaying cabin. Frank is covered in sweat and out of breath.

Frank

Who the Fuck would be living out here?

Bill responds with a sarcastic smile.

Bill

Maybe your hairy girlfriend lives there?

Frank

Once again, who is jealous of my Bigfoot sex romp? That would be you.

Bill points towards the front of the cabin.

Bill

It's probably an old hunting cabin. Look at the brush all overgrown around the cabin, yet it's all matted down walking up to the cabin.

Frank

So?

Bill

It means someone has been here. By the looks of it, I would say recently.

Quoteboy rubs hand sanitizer on his fingers.

Quoteboy

I won't say it but its "highly" probably that the Elite Democratic Hitman Squad has been here.

Bill

Not Hitmen but someone.

Frank

Maybe not a someone. Maybe a something.

Bill

Now who sounds like a line from a Bruce Willis movie?

Frank

Yeh that was kind of Bruce Willisie.

Bill

Totally but in a good way.

Frank

You can never overdose on too much Bruce Willis.

Quoteboy

Again with "this" Bruce Willis person. He sounds like an Alt Left Operative looking to take down Donald Trump "Junior" in some Trump Tower scandal. Am I correct?

Bill

No.

Quoteboy

Was "I" close?

Bill

No.

Quoetboy

You know the Trump children have the highest IQ's ever "recorded" by Science. It's a Trath.

Bill

Did you just seriously say that out loud?

Quoteboy

"I" did.

Bill

Just stop talking. Please.

Bill walks towards the front of the cabin and is slowly followed by Frank. Bill steps on the small wooden porch skipping over the rotted wooden planks. He reaches for the split log wooden door and pushes it inward. He enters the cabin slowly.

Frank

This place is a dump. Someone needs to make a Home Depot run for Flip This Shack.

Bill

Watch your step. You weigh more than this entire cabin.

Frank stops Bill from moving by grabbing his arm and sarcastically replies.

Frank

Haha, a fat joke. So original and witty.

Quoteboy

You know guys "maybe we" should rethink entering this cabin.

Bill turns to Quoteboy.

Bill

I know I am going to regret asking this but why should we rethink going into this cabin?

Quoteboy rubs hand sanitizer on his fingers.

Quoteboy

What if it is full of Crisis "Actors to" stage a mass shooting scene to defame the NRA? Or worse, to make Eric Trump look incompetent. Has that ever "crossed" your Liberal minds?

Bill

No.

Frank

Not at all.

Quoteboy

Well I feel we should think about it "before we" step in there. This could 'be" the start of World War Three. Just ask Alex.

Bill and Frank speak at the same time.

Bill & Frank

Shut the Fuck up.

Bill enters the cabin and is followed by Frank and Quoteboy. The floor boards creek as Frank steps on them. Quoteboy takes out his digital thermometer scanner and scans the room.

CHAPTER FIVE - FOUND THE BUTTER STICK

Day. Interior. Cabin.

Bill, Quoteboy and Frank have entered the cabin. It's completely baron of any items except an old wooden table in the center of the floor accompanied by three old wooden chairs with peeling white paint and a pot belly stove. There are four walls, the front door and a side window on the left wall that is missing its glass. The roof has a huge hole in it that is letting in some daylight that is shining down onto the table. Bill Points to what is on the table.

Bill

I found your butter stick.

Frank looks at his stick of butter sitting on the table.

Frank

How the Fuck did that get here?

Bill looks at Frank and then turns to Quoteboy.

Bill

I don't know and Quoteboy if you say some Democratic Hitmen Bullshit I will slap the quotes out of your fingers.

Quoteboy makes the motion of locking his lips with a key and tossing the key away.

Frank

Seriously how did it Fucking get here? If I lost it, it would have fallen out behind us and yet it is now in front of us. So someone put it on that Grandma looking kitchen table.

Bill

Maybe your new hairy girlfriend found it and was going to bake you a cake in her lovely rotting wood condo.

Frank points his finger at Bill in disgust.

Frank

Shut up that's really not funny. This is seriously creeping me out. I need a candy bar.

Bill

No, you want a candy bar.

Frank

No I need a candy bar. My doctor says it's like medicine for me.

Bill

I seriously doubt there is an actual doctor who would prescribe Snicker's bars.

Frank reaches into his pillow case and rummages around until he pulls out a Charlston Chew candy bar. He opens it quickly and begins chomping on it. Bill walks around the cabin as Frank eats his last candy bar and then all three of them hear fast movement through the trees and brush like something is running around the cabin.

Frank

What the Fuck is that?

Bill turns towards the front door.

Bill

Something big.

Quoteboy takes out his digital thermometer scanner and scans the walls and follows the sounds. Bill catches a glimpse of a shadow running past the window on the left hand wall and follows it as it moves around the cabin and then the sound stops at the right hand wall. Bill motions to Frank to be quiet and mouths the words "Stay still". Bill slowly walks towards the right hand wall as he carefully steps over the rotted wooden floor planks. Bill reaches the wall and just listens. Bill can hear Frank chomping on his candy bar so he turns his head towards Frank and makes the "Shhh" motion with his finger and lips. Quoteboy uses his digital

thermometer scanner and scans the walls.
Bill turns his head back towards the wall
and then a loud animal like scream can be
heard, followed by the sound of running and
breaking branches. Frank drops his candy
bar as Bill runs out of the cabin and runs
towards the sound and stops as he watches
the tree branches and brush in the distance
move in the pattern of a person or animal
running through them. Then it just stops.
Frank grabs the butter stick off of the table
and places it in his front pants pocket and
then exits the cabin and tries to quickly
move in Bill's direction. He stops when he
reaches Bill as he is out of breath.

Frank

I know I have said this a lot on this trip, but what the Fuck was that?

Bill

I'm guessing your hairy girlfriend. Take a whiff of the air. It smells like moldy cheese and old lady clothes.

Quoteboy

Whatever it was "it" had a temperature of 104.6. Too hot to "be" a Republican.

Frank snorts the air.

Frank

Fuck it's her. Maybe she's looking for some more lovin' with the Frankster. Once the honey's taste this, they all want seconds. That would explain her hot body temp.

Bill turns and stares at Frank.

Bill

I doubt that scream was a mating call. It sounded pretty pissed off to me. Did you two have a lover's quarrel? What you couldn't agree on style of window drapes from Crate and Barrel?

Frank

Damn your just full of zingers today.

Bill

I try.

Quoteboy

Maybe she just wants to come back and review your medical "records to" make sure you don't have any communicable diseases or check your "Registered Voting" status.

Frank glares at Quoteboy.

Frank

I am a registered Independent.

Quoteboy rubs hand sanitizer on his fingers.

Quoteboy

I cannot believe I "am" friends with you.

Frank

Who said we were friends?

Bill

Enough you two.

Frank

Maybe she just really, really wanted to eat my butter stick.

Bill shakes his head from side to side and walks back towards the cabin.

Bill

If that's the case, then you two deserve each other.

Quoteboy removes his hat and wipes the sweat away from his forehead with his Paul Ryan face embossed hanky.

Quoteboy

I would not strive to "develop a" relationship with this female Bigfoot. The chances of it being "a" meaningful and successful relationship are slim at best.

Frank

Why because I am fat?

Quoteboy

No because she obviously has "a" deeper level "of intelligence" than you.

Frank yells and points at Quoteboy.

Frank

Your President is still Fucking Orange!

Bill

Enough you two.

Frank

So what now?

Bill

I guess we just wait.

Quoteboy

Oh I know, we can pass "the time" by playing the "If you had to pick one game." Frank you "go" first.

Frank smiles.

Frank

Quoteboy, if you had to pick one, would you rather Fuck Alex Jones up the ass after a night of Taco Bell or Fuck a hole in a pine tree?

Quoteboy

I am not a homosexual so the "question" has no relevance to me.

Frank

Shut the Fuck up and answer.

Quoteboy rubs hand sanitizer on his fingers.

Quoteboy

I would prefer "sexual" intercourse with Alex over a tree.

Frank

Bill?

Bill

I would totally Fuck the tree.

Frank

I would Fuck that tree twice and coat the branches with my baby gravy.

Quoteboy

What is Baby Gravy? Is it 'made" by Gerber?

Frank

I can make you some right now. Give me like seven minutes.

Bill starts to laugh as Quoteboy looks confused.

Quoteboy

I don't understand.

Frank

It's right here in my pants. Let me whip you up a batch.

Frank unzips his pants and laughs.

Quoteboy

So your Baby Batter is "just a way" for you to reference your semen. That is pretty odd if you ask me.

Frank

It's funny. Lighten the Fuck up.

Quoteboy

I just do not see the humor in in. Bill, do you find this humorous?

Bill laughs

Bill

Yeh it's pretty funny.

Quoteboy

I do not find "it" funny and do you know what else I do not find funny?

Bill

I am going to regret this but what else do you not find funny?

Quoteboy

Democratic Congressman "who in" the middle of the night, throw rolls of toilet paper into the trees "on" the lawns of the homes of Republican Senators.

Bill

Why did I invite you on this trip?

CHAPTER SIX - MAYBE SHE WANTS SECONDS?

Night. Interior. Cabin.

Frank, Quoteboy and Bill are sitting at the old wooden table in the cabin. The pot belly stove has a roaring fire that is lighting up the cabin. The chair that Frank is sitting on is creaking loudly.

Frank

Explain to me again why we are spending another night out here and not driving home in the F-150 with leather seats and air conditioning?

Bill points to Frank's chair as he eats a protein bar.

Bill

Your chair is going to break.

Frank sarcastically replies.

Frank

Haha, another fat joke. I get it. Fat guy on an old wooden chair. Would could go wrong.

Quoteboy

Statistically, when an overweight person sits on a wooden "chair that" has been exposed to the yearly elements such as the chair that you "are" sitting on, well the chair just "Fucking" breaks.

Frank wiggles his bottle from side to side.

Frank

All good.

The chair legs snap off and Frank falls to the floor of the cabin.

Bill

I told you.

Frank struggles to get up but then decides to just sit on the floor.

Frank

You didn't answer my question. Why are we here for another night?

Bill

We went far too deep into the woods today. We never would have walked out before nightfall. This is a shelter so we will use it.

Quoteboy

I agree. As a "former" Safety Officer and current Treasurer of the Jeff Sessions Fan Club, I feel this is "the best course" of action. Especially if the woods are crawling with Democratic Hitmen.

Frank looks up from the floor and gets serious.

Frank

I wasn't always fat you know. I got fat in the sixth grade when my Mom died. The doctors say is was a coping mechanism. I remember it started after the funeral. We had this huge buffet at our house. I vividly recall thinking to myself, why are we having a party at the house after Mom died? I was just a kid I didn't understand how funerals worked but understood food. I attacked that buffet and never turned back.

Bill

If you don't make a change Frank, you probably won't live to see Thirty. It's that simple.

Quoteboy

It is in "the statistics" Frank. By my calculations you will be dead in 237 days.

Frank

I know. I want to change I really do it's just not that easy. I want to be healthy and fit. I want to be that guy. You know the guy that gets the girl. Right now all I can get is raped by a Bigfoot. I was sound asleep when that thing started Fucking me. When I did wake I was too damn scared to move. It really hurt.

I felt my Dick was going to break off and that smell. God that Fucking smell.

Bill

like moldy cheese and old lady clothes.

Frank lets out a short laugh and a smirk.

Frank

Yeh, like moldy cheese and old lady clothes.

Bill and Frank both laugh. Quoteboy just glares at the both of them as he applies hand sanitizer to his fingers and adjusts his hat.

Quoteboy

"Was" that humorous? I don't get it.

Frank

 So what now?

Bill

We wait for daylight and hike back.

A loud scream can be heard outside the cabin followed by a loud thump against the cabin door. Frank, Quoteboy and Bill turn to look at the cabin door as it violently shakes and then stops.

Frank

Once again, what the Fuck was that?

Bill

Maybe your hairy girlfriend wants seconds?

Frank points at Bill with anger.

Frank

No time for jokes this is Fuckin serious here. I do not want to die in a cabin in the woods like some B-horror movie.

Frank quickly changes his tone from anger to curiosity as he combs his hair with his fingers.

Frank (continued)

She probably does want seconds. Once you have Frank in ya stank tank you want nothing else.

Bill just rolls his eyes and shakes his head from side to side as he stands up and walks towards the front door with his knife is his right hand. He stops just before the door. All that can be heard is crickets in the woods outside of the cabin and then all the crickets go silent.

Frank (continued)

The woods are silent until they're not? Right? Well it just got pretty Fucking silent out there.

Bill turns towards Frank and gestures to him to be quiet. Frank makes the motion of locking his lips and throwing away the key. Quoteboy gives Frank the thumbs up symbol as Bill turns back towards the door as the rusty door latch and handle begin to move. The door latch can be heard unclicking as the creaking wooden door slowly opens inward as a large man with a scruffy beard and layers of tattered clothes holding a dead squirrel in his hand enters the cabin.

Mitch

Why the Fuck are you in my house?

Bill

We didn't think anyone lived here. We just needed a place to stay for the night.

Mitch looks down at the floor and sees his broken chair and then looks at Frank.

Mitch

You broke my chair Fat Boy?

Mitch looks back towards Bill.

Mitch (continued)

And you Rambo, you can put your city knife away. Where did you get that? probably at Bass Pro shops or some other Shit corporate retailer.

Bill puts his knife away as Mitch walks up to the table and drops down his dead squirrel to the floor.

Frank

You have a really nice place.

Mitch

Are you Fucking with me Fat Boy?

Frank

No sir.

Mitch looks at Quoteboy.

Mitch

And you, you look like an L.L. Bean catalog model.

Bill lets out a laugh.

Quoteboy

I have already heard "that" recently but thank you "for" the observation.

Mitch glares at Quoteboy as he makes air quotes with his fingers.

Mitch

Why are you air quoting?

Quoteboy begins to answer but is cut off by Bill.

Bill

Don't ask. The answer is far too long. So this is a pretty run down shack. You can't really live here.

Mitch

Didn't your mother ever tell you not to insult a man's home? There is more than meets the eye here.

Mitch places his hand under the table and pulls a latch and then flips the table upward along with a trap door in the floor. He grabs his squirrel and begins to climb down the stairs in the floor. He looks back up towards Frank and Bill.

Mitch (continued)

Fat boy and Rambo, are you coming? You too Quotefingers.

Mitch walks down the stairs and lights can be seen turning on as Frank stares at Bill and then sarcastically speaks.

Frank

Sure, let's follow the creepy Mountain Man down to the secret room under his cabin. What the Fuck could go wrong?

Quoteboy rubs hand sanitizer on his fingers.

Quoteboy

Statistically, a lot "could" go wrong.

Bill starts to climb down the stairs followed by Quoteboy and then Frank. Frank gets stuck in the narrow opening and tries to force himself down the stairway. Bill Looks back up at Frank.

Bill

What the Fuck are you doing Frank?

Frank struggles to move but he is stuck.

Frank

I'm stuck.

Bill

What do you mean you are stuck?

Frank again struggles to free himself but he cannot.

Frank

I'm stuck. This opening is small.

Mitch looks back up the staircase and speaks.

Mitch

No you are stuck because you are a Fat Boy.

Quoteboy

This unshaven smelly Mountain Man is correct. "You" are obese.

Frank struggles and finally gets free and is able to descend the stairs.

CHAPTER SEVEN- FATBOY FRANK, QUOTEFINGERS & RAMBO

Night. Interior. Bunker.

Mitch is sitting in a leather Lazy Boy recliner filling his pipe with Tobacco and smoking it while Frank, Quoteboy and Bill are sitting on an upholstered sofa in an underground concrete and metal bunker. Mitch is just starring at Frank and Bill. Frank nervously starts to talk and leans forward on the couch.

Frank

That's a nice recliner you have. My Dad has one just like it. Does that have the massage option? My Dad's does, it's pretty cool.

Mitch

It does.

Frank

That's a nice pipe it's like the one Sherlock Holmes had, you know the English FBI guy.

Quoteboy

Sherlock "Holmes" wasn't in the FBI. He was a fictional English Detective in 1887. The American FBI "wasn't" formed until 1908 so statistically it is impossible that he was in the FBI.

Frank elbows Quoteboy as Mitch relights his pipe as he looks directly at Bill.

Mitch

Tell me Rambo, do these two always talk this much?

Bill

Pretty much. And the name's Bill not Rambo. Bill with a B.

Frank

Why do you live under your cabin like a hobbit?

Mitch lowers his pipe and leans forward from his Lazy Boy recliner and raises his voice.

Mitch

Why not.

Frank rolls his eyes and sits back on the couch as Bill looks around the bunker and sees that it is well stocked with supplies amenities and the walls have drawings of bigfoot hanging up with a map and pushpins.

Bill

Your tracking Bigfoot?

Mitch leans back in his Lazy Boy recliner.

Mitch

You ask too many questions. Why are you three here again?

Bill

Our hike took longer than planned. We hit a snag and needed a place to crash for the night.

Frank

It's because I Fucked Bigfoot.

Bill elbows Frank in the gut and gives him a dirty look as Mitch leans forward in his Lazy Boy recliner.

Mitch

Come again?

Frank

Nothing.

Mitch

No, no, no Fat Boy. You said you Fucked Bigfoot. Now I am not sure how that took place, seeing how your Fatly Obese and probably haven't visually seen your own Cock in my guess would be nine years.

Frank becomes defensive and sarcastic.

Frank

My name is Frank. And I see my Cock everyday thank you Sherlock Holmes.

Mitch

I'm Mitch. Tell me Fat boy Frank. Were you asleep and woke up to her hairy smelly thick body riding your Cock?

Bill and Frank both look at each other and then look at Mitch.

Frank

How did you know that?

Mitch

It's their mating season. It's what she does. It happened to me in the summer of 99. Tell me, did the Pussy smell like fancy ass French cheese?

Frank

Yeh, moldy cheese and old lady clothes.

Quoteboy raises his hand.

Quoteboy

I slept through "the" supposed encounter but I did wake to smell moldy cheese and Frank's half erection. Just for "the" record.

Frank elbows Quoteboy in the shoulder.

Mitch

How long ago did this happen and where?

Frank points to the wall.

Frank

Yesterday. In the woods back a bit.

Bill

It was three miles west of here.

Mitch

She's branching out. Traveling farther than usual.

Bill looks on the wall behind Mitch and sees a calendar from 2001.

Bill

How long have you been down here?

Mitch

I built this in the fall of 2000. Right after my encounter with Bessy.

Bill

Bessy?

Mitch

I named the Bigfoot. I felt it deserved a name being a female and all. I haven't seen any males in years. Just the one female. I don't care for people much so that's why I live down here. Passers bye, even thou they are few and far between just think it's an old rundown hunter's cabin and they pass right on by. Except you three. Quotefingers, Fat Boy Frank and Rambo.

Frank

Hey after the first time when she, you know Fucked you. Did it happen again? Like a second or third time, maybe different positions, maybe Doggy style? Would a Bigfoot call it Doggy style? I don't know?

Mitch

Nope. One and done. From what I can gather she just does it during mating season and since there are no male Bigfoots left around here, she goes after the next best replacement, man. You were nothing but nature's sperm bank to her.

Bill looks at Frank and smiles as he whispers.

Bill

I guess she wasn't coming back for seconds.

Frank sticks his fingers in Bills face.

Frank

Smell my fingers.

Quoteboy

Why "would" you want him to smell your fingers? Is that humorous?

Bill swats Frank's hand away from his face as Mitch reaches for something behind his chair.

Mitch

I found a Twinkie by the Bleeding Spruce Trees. Was that yours Fat Boy Frank?

Frank becomes defensive and plays dumb.

Frank

Nope. Who would take Twinkies on a hike. That is ridiculous.

Quoteboy rubs hand sanitizer on his fingers.

Quoteboy

Well statistically "it" most likely is yours Frank. The odds of the said Twinkie belonging to "another" overweight hiker are very remote.

Frank elbows Quoteboy as Mitch tosses Frank the unopened Twinkie.

Mitch

I guess it belonged to another Fat Boy out here roaming these woods. Like Quotefingers said, what are the odds of that?

Frank nervously shakes his head yes.

Frank

Yeh odd chance but it must be.

Mitch points to Frank's T shirt.

Mitch

You like Tupac?

Frank looks down at his T shirt then back up towards Mitch.

Frank

Of course. Who doesn't. The man was a genius.

Mitch begins to rap a Tupac lyric.

Mitch

I'm just a Black Man caught up in the mix tryin' to make a dollar outa fifteen cents, a Dime and a Nickle.

Frank smiles.

Frank

 Did you seriously just rap some Tupac?

Frank looks at Bill and pushes his shoulder.

Frank (continued)

My boy underground Mitch got some mad skills son.

Bill looks at Frank and shakes his head from side to side and replies to Frank with false enthusiasm.

Bill

Yeh. He's got it all right.

Quoteboy

I didn't like it. The "so" called flow was all off beat. I'm sorry Mitch but you will most likely never have a "career as" a professional rap artist.

Frank elbows Quoteboy in the side.

Frank

I Get Around. Great song. More of a party song not a statement song but none the less, great tune.

Mitch

I have been known to spit some truth from time to time. I have a theory on who actually killed Tupac.

Bill sits back as Quoteboy and Frank lean forward.

Frank

No Fucking way? I would love to hear your theory.

Quoteboy

"Indeed."

Mitch

I believe it was the Government using an elite squad of Democratic assassins or hitmen if you will.

Quoteboy smiles and gives Mitch a thumbs up.

Frank

Come again?

Mitch

The Democrats have captured and bred Bigfoots in captivity to carry out some of mankind's greatest assassinations. Both Kennedy brothers, Martin Luther King, Abe Lincoln, Tupac and Biggie. The list goes on and on.

Mitch leans forward in his Lazy Boy recliner and Quoetboy has a confused expression on his face.

Mitch(continued)

They have a 5000-acre training facility under The Kennedy compound on Cape Cod. I covertly found my way into the sewer system there and located the facility myself. I lived in that sewer system for the entire month of April 2004. It was the best time to go, being tax season and all. You see Bigfoot isn't a myth. It is a super engineered killing machine that can travel across dimensions and shape shift. All curtesy of your United States government. Well the Democratic half anyway.

Quoetboy

I followed you 100% with "the" Democratic Hitmen but you lost me when "you" tossed a shape shifting dimension traveling Bigfoot "into" the equation.

Bill looks up on the shelf to the right of the map and sees an array of prescription pill bottles so he tries to change the conversation.

Bill

Hey Mitch, do you take any medications?

Mitch

I did back in 1999. They said I suffered from delusions and reality belief issues. Fuck them I say. Fancy ass Democratic New York city doctors. What the Fuck do they know. Right Fat Boy?

Frank nervously replies with what he thinks Mitch wants to hear.

Frank

Yeh, Fuck them. Damn the man!

Quoteboy

Mitch is on to something. The Democratic National Convention "has long" been behind experimental reality altering buffet foods served during the conventions. It is fact. I am not 100% sold on the Bigfoot shape shifting dimension traveling theory but I am sure Alex Jones will look into it and prove it as Alternative Fact Trath.

Mitch

You listen to Alex Jones too?

Quoteboy

"Religiously every" night after my mom tucks me in in my basement apartment bed.

Frank

It's creepy, you're a grown up adult and you still sleep on your childhood bed with your Star Wars sheets.

Mitch

I have all of his episodes recorded onto 8-Track tape. You see the Deep State can't trace old 8-track tape recordings. And for your information Frank, I still sleep on my childhood mattress.

Frank

But your like old. So your mattress would be like really old. That's kinda gross.

Mitch

It's a sixty-nine-year-old mattress. The Government can't track it that is why I keep it.

Frank

You and Quoteboy have to be related somehow.

Quoteboy

I have also heard that Democrats try to listen to us by placing "listening" devices in our Bump Stocks.

Mitch

I like how you think Quotefingers and If you need to know Rambo, I haven't touched one of those pills in years and I have never been in better touch with reality.

Frank pretends to yawn to change the conversation.

Frank

Ok well I am all conspiracy theory'd out. Hey we are like super tired. Do you mind if we crash now and get some shuteye?

Bill

Yes, let's do that.

Mitch

I only sleep forty-four minutes a night. Anymore sleep and you are not a man in my book. You're a Pussy.

Frank

Well I guess I am a big pink juicy Pussy because I really like sleeping.

Mitch

Suit yourself. Pussy.

Bill

So are we cool to sleep here?

Mitch

You three can stay the night but after breakfast I want you gone. I will be making Squirrel and forest potatoes. That couch pulls out into a bed. And the Lazyboy reclines pretty far and is damn comfortable. I'll be in the back bedroom. If you steal anything in the middle of the night, I will find you Fat Boy Frank, Quotefingers and Rambo and I will gut you with your own Bass Pro Shop knife.

Mitch stands up and begins to walk towards a door. He pauses to place a new push pin into his map on the wall and then he opens the door, enters the room and closes the door behind him. As soon as the door shuts Frank rips open the Twinkie and eats it with one bite. Bill looks at Frank with disgust as he shakes his head from side to side.

Quoteboy

I liked Mitch "until" he threw in the Bigfoot hitman theory. Coo –Coo.

Quoteboy makes the crazy symbol with his fingers twirling next to his head.

Frank

Did you seriously just call him crazy? You are pretty Fucking nuts yourself. You and Mitch seem related to me. Didn't your Dad leave you and your Mom when you were like six years old? Maybe Mitch is your Dad.

Quoteboy rubs hand sanitizer on his fingers.

Quoteboy

I have been "certified" sane. I have the medical documents if you would like to glance over "them" and Mitch cannot be my biological Father. My biological Father's first name "was" not Mitch it was Angus. His middle name was Mitch.

Quoteboy reaches in his backpack and hands Frank a manila envelope.

Frank

That is what I am talking about. Who would take those documents on a Fucking hike? This is an overnight hike not a Fucking Doctor's visit. Bill help me here. Please.

Bill

I'm going to bed.

Quoteboy frantically looks through his backpack.

Quoteboy

Has anyone "seen my" Jeff Sessions doll? I cannot find him? I can't sleep without Jeff. Where is my Jeff? Jeff? Jeff? Jeff?

CHAPTER EIGHT - NO CRICKETS

Day. Exterior. Woods.

Frank, Quoteboy and Bill are walking through the woods. Frank is covered in sweat and out of breath.

Frank

I can't believe I ate squirrel for breakfast and it was pretty fucking good.

Bill

Has there ever been anything you didn't eat that was put in front of your face?

Frank

Good point. Hey you know for a creepy mountain man, Mitch turned out to be an OK dude. I never would have guessed he was into Tupac. How Fucked up was that.

Bill

Less talking more walking.

Quoteboy

I found it to be stringy "and" unpleasant to eat. I still have fur in my throat.

Frank

Do you think we will see her on the way back?

Bill pauses and stops walking and turns back towards Frank.

Bill

I don't know. Do you miss your hairy lover? Maybe you two can text back and forth and use cute smiley face emoji's or maybe she's on Facebook and she will send you a friend request.

Frank raises his fingers and sticks them in Bill's face.

Frank

Smell my fingers. That Bessy stank is still on there.

Bill swats Franks hand away from his face.

Bill

Wow now you're calling her Bessy?

Frank

That is her name. Are you jealous that I got laid on this trip and you didn't? smell my fingers.

Frank raises his fingers and sticks them in Bill's face. Bill swats Franks hand away from his face and then stops moving and looks around.

Frank (continued)

What is it?

Bill

The crickets stopped.

Frank and Bill turn back to back and look all around 360 degrees into the woods but see nothing. Bill unsnaps his knife pouch and takes about five steps away from Frank and focuses on some brush in the woods. He squints his eyes to try and get a better look.

Frank

Do you see something? What is it?

Quoteboy

Is it "the" Democratic Hitmen?

The crickets start chirping again as Bill turns back around to face Frank as he replies.

Bill

It's nothing.

Frank

You sure?

Bill

I just said it's nothing.

Frank

Yeh but are you sure?

Bill

Probably just a squirrel. If we catch it, you can have lunch.

Frank sarcastically replies.

Frank

Wow another fat joke.

Bill

No that was a backwoods Hillbilly I will eat any critter joke.

Frank

Funny. Really great stuff. I close my eyes and swear you are Chris Rock. No, no, I mean Richard Fucking Pryor.

Bill

But you would eat it. Admit it. You would it another squirrel I we caught one.

Frank

Maybe.

Quoteboy

Who "is" Richard Fucking Pryor?

Bill and Frank glare at Quoteboy with disbelief.

Bill

It's like you have lived half your life under a rock.

Frank

No it is more like he was born at the age of nineteen and missed the first nineteen years of life. I am Fucking starving. Give me one of those Glucose IV bags.

Quoteboy rubs hand sanitizer on his fingers.

Quoteboy

I will give you "some" instructions on how to properly administer this IV. There is an SOP that needs to "be" followed for cleanliness and general safety concerns.

Quoteboy reaches in his backpack and hands Frank an IV bag. Frank quickly grabs it and bites the end to tear it open and drinks it like a bottle of beer.

Frank

Not bad.

Quoteboy

Biting it and "drinking it like" a Coors Light was not in the SOP.

Frank burps very loud and tosses the empty IV bag back to Quoteboy.

Frank

Whatever dude.

Quoteboy

Whatever dude? SOP's are put in place for specific reasons Frank. To "ignore an" SOP is like ignoring the "Second" Amendment of the constitution.

Frank

Isn't that the Right to Eat Pussy?

Frank and Bill begin to laugh as Quoteboy gets angry.

Quoteboy

No Frank it is "the" Right to Bear Arms.

The crickets stop chirping again as Frank then notices directly behind Bill stands what appears to be a Bigfoot. Seven feet tall covered in long stringy hair with visible hanging breasts. Frank turns white as a ghost as he points towards Bill as his body shakes.

Bill

What the Fuck is wrong with you?

Frank

No crickets.

Bill turns his head back over his shoulder and is hit from behind and falls hard to the ground and blacks out.

CHAPTER NINE – I WANT THE BUTTER BACK

Day. Exterior. Woods.

Frank is staring up at the female Bigfoot as she takes a step towards him. Frank is frozen with fear and just stands there. She takes another step towards him and begins to sniff around him. Quoteboy faints and falls to the ground.

Frank

I guess to you I probably smell huh?

The Bigfoot just stares at Frank and then raises her left arm and uses her index finger to point towards Frank.

Frank (continued)

Are you pointing at me? Do you remember me?

Frank starts to talk in basic tones like he is talking to a dumb person. He looks and sees Bessy Bigfoot has Quoteboy's Jeff Sessions doll in her left hand.

Frank (continued)

Me Frank. You Bigfoot. I come in peace. You like doll. Doll is good. You keep doll. Fuck Quoteboy.

The Bigfoot lets out a grunt and continues to point towards Frank. Frank begins to relax a little bit and speak with swagger.

Frank (continued)

Yeh that's it. You remember the Frankster. Once you have some Frank in yo stank tank you can never forget. All the honeys want Frank even the big hairy Honeys. Hey are you pointing at my Dick? You dirty girl, you dirty, dirty hairy girl. you want a second helping of the Frank experience don't you? But do me a favor can you toss the Jeff Sessions doll? That thing seriously Fucking creeps me out.

The Bigfoot lets out a grunt and continues to point towards Frank. Frank begins to unzip his pants.

Frank (continued)

Yeh Mountain Man Mitch said you were a one and done but obvious you want a little somethin' somethin' from the Frankster.

The Bigfoot lets out a louder grunt and places her pointing finger against Frank's pants pocket. Frank looks down at his pocket with a confused expression on his face.

Frank (continued)

You want my pocket?

The Bigfoot lets out a much louder grunt and uses her pointing finger and pokes Frank's pants pocket.

Frank (continued)

You want what's in the pocket? I'm confused. Damn I wish you could speak my language.

Frank speaks softly down towards Quoteboy.

Frank (continued)

Quoteboy get up. You have to see this.

Frank reaches in his pocket and pulls out a half melted stick of butter. The Bigfoot grabs the butter stick from Frank's hand and lets out a loud scream and then turns around and runs back into the woods. Frank is left just standing there with butter dripping from his hand and his pants unzipped.

Frank (continued)

Wait. Come back. Come back. Will I see you again? Can I give you my number? Do you use Skype?

CHAPTER TEN – QUOTEBBOY ORIGINS

Day. Exterior. Woods.

Quoteboy is waking up from passing out as Frank is just gazing into the woods dripping with butter from his hand and his fly open.

Quoteboy

"What" happened?

Frank

Bill got clocked in the head by Bessy. You passed out like a little Bitch and I manned up and went down on her. Yeh, that's right I ate that Bigfoot Pussy. Front to back like it was a rare Roast Beef sandwich.

Quoteboy

"One" word, Bacteria. Did you actually do that?

Frank hesitates then responds.

Frank

No but I could have. She stole my butter stick and ran away.

Quoteboy

I "assumed" as much.

Frank

Do you ever not do the air quote thing?

Quoteboy

I do it all "the" time. Even when "I" dream.

Frank

Why?

Quoteboy

Most people think I am just a "freak for" doing it. I get that. in some ways I guess I am. I know I am different.

Quoteboy pauses and looks away.

Frank

Hey if you don't want to tell me it's cool. Whatever dude.

Quoteboy

We were "sitting" around the kitchen table having blueberry pancakes. My mom would always use fresh not frozen blueberries. On this particular morning she didn't have any fresh blueberries so she had no choice but to use frozen. My Dad who was a man of few words sat down at the 'kitchen table" cut his pancakes left to right as he always did and took a medium sized bite, no syrup needed. He then proceeded to spit them out onto the floor and ask my mother what the "Fuck are these?" She replied blueberry pancakes. He stood up and using air quotes he said "blueberry pancakes?" no these are not "blueberry pancakes" these are "Shit", your "Shit" and this snot nosed kid is "Shit" with his Conspiracy Theories! I'm out of here. He walked out of the kitchen and then the house. We never saw him again. I starting "Air Quoting" right after that. My Mom would later tell me that my Dad had some mental issues and considered himself a Bigfoot Hunter which fascinated me as a child but that didn't change the fact he just left us.

Frank

What a Fucking Dick.

Quoteboy wipes his nose and eyes.

Quoteboy

I would agree "he was very" Penis like.

Frank

So it was like a coping thing? Kinda like me and food after my Mom died.

Quoteboy

Yes. Except I don't eat at the buffet "table" like a pig at the trough.

Frank

Fuck you. You and I actually have something in common. Now that's a Conspiracy Theory for ya right there. So your Dad was a Fucking Bigfoot hunter and we are out here in the woods and I banged a Bigfoot. Small Fucking world. Alright that explains that. What about the whole Conspiracy Theory Shit and crazy Democrats and yada yada.

Quoteboy

What about it?

Frank

When did you start believing in it?

Quoteboy

I came out of my Mother's womb as "a Republican baby" with a Conservative agenda.

Frank

Why do you do it? Why do you believe in that Shit?

Quoteboy

"Because" it's all Trath.

Frank

Trath is not a real Fucking word. What the Fuck is wrong with you. It's made up.

Quoteboy

Typical response from a "Bleeding Heart Liberal" who believes in saving the environment, animal rights, Human rights and who doesn't want the "Wall."

Frank gets heated, loud and angry.

Frank

None of what you just said has Shit to do with what we were talking about. Shit.

Quoteboy begins to chant and fist pump the air in between air quoting.

Quoteboy

Lock "her" up! Lock her up! "Lock" her up!

Frank

Again, nothing to do with the conversation.

Quoteboy

Alex says people like you give answers like that "because you" cannot handle the Trath.

Frank

I think I really understand now why your Dad left. If I was Dad, I would have taken you on a Bigfoot hunt and gave you to

Bigfoot to eat like a burger. I would have thrown in some lettuce, pickles and ketchup. Two bites, all gone.

Quoteboy

"Fake" News.

Frank

Your President is still Orange. Boom!

Quoteboy

I would love to continue this "witty banter but" I suggest we get Bill to a hospital.

Frank looks down at Bill. Bill is still unconscious laying in the dirt with a huge bump on his head.

Frank.

I actually agree with you on something. Can you get us out of here?

Quoteboy

Of course I can. I am "a Republican with" an Agenda.

Frank

That means Shit. All that tells me is your Anti- Abortion and wear really bad suits.

Quoteboy

I have a sense of direction like a pregnant Hawk on a "nutrition" mission. If you want to get out "of here, follow" Quoteboy.

CHAPTER ELEVEN - WHAT THE FUCK DUDE

Day. Interior. Hospital.

Bill is waking up in a hospital bed. He is dazed and confused as he opens his eyes and sees Frank and Quoteboy sitting next to him. Frank is eating a hot dog. Frank realizes that Bill is waking up so he jams the rest of the hot dog in his mouth as Quoteboy leans towards Bill with his digital thermometer and takes his body temperature.

Quoteboy

"Welcome" back.

Frank

Dude your awake. I thought we lost you there for a while. How you feel?

Bill

Like I have the worst hangover known to man. What the Fuck happened to me?

Frank

You know, Bessy slammed you hard in the head. You went down like a whore on Saturday night.

Bill tries to sit upright and lean against his pillows.

Bill

Bessy? Who the Hell is Bessy?

Frank

You know Bessy. My hairy girlfriend.

Bill

No clue what you are talking about?

Frank

What the Fuck dude? What do you mean? You don't remember?

Bill

The last thing I can remember was being in work Friday.

Frank

Your Fucking with us right?

Bill

No. that's all I remember. Why are you here anyway?

Frank

Why am I here? Dude, me, you and Quoteboy went on an overnight hike that turned into a few days and I fucked a Bigfoot.

Bill smiles as he leans forward.

Bill

Now you are Fucking with me.

Quoteboy

I can assure you "he" is not Fucking with you.

Frank

What the Fuck dude. You seriously don't remember what we went through?

Bill

No.

Frank

None of it?

Bill

No.

Frank

Not the woods are silent until they're not Bullshit?

Bill

No.

Quoteboy rubs hand sanitizer on his fingers.

Quoteboy

It's "the" Damn Democratic Hitmen. They got to Bill. They got to him.

Frank

What about meeting Mountain Man Mitch and his underground creepy cave house and his love of Tupac?

Bill

No.

Frank

At the campfire you bitched at me for bringing 24 pack of Twinkies on a hike. You have to remember that?

Bill

No.

Frank

You watched me, Frank bang a big hairy smelly female bigfoot. You have to remember that. Think hard. Really Fucking hard.

Bill begins to laugh.

Bill

It sounds like you're the one that hit their Fucking head.

Frank stands up and begins to get heated and angry.

Frank

Dude it happened. I banged a female Bigfoot. Right in our campsite. What the Fuck dude. I even stuck my fingers in your face so you could sniff the worst smelling Pussy ever. You don't remember it smelled like moldy cheese and old lady clothes?

Bill stops laughing and tries to be serious.

Bill

Frank if you say so then good for you. I'm glad you got laid. By a Bigfoot.

Quoteboy

This is a conspiracy of epic proportions. Bill, other than your unexplained time loss, do you feel like you were "probed" by Men in Black? Which is just Democratic Governors covertly working for the CIA. Maybe Frank's Bigfoot encounter never happened, maybe it was memory placement from Hilary's inner circle to take "focus" away from the Liberal agenda. I can only assume that this hospital is full "of" Crisis Actors from Central Casting. Frank, do you have unexplained memory loss? Have you seen "this" Bigfoot in any news film footage of mass shootings? Please tell me you are not drinking the tap water. Do you know "what mind" altering drugs the Democrats put in our tap water? Oh for the love of God please tell me your parents didn't vaccinate you as a child? You know the Democrats "engineered the" chemical compound of those vaccinations to change your thought process to not vote Republican. And don't even "get" me started on Operation Mockingbird and the Fake Media. Frank tell me, do you understand what "Q" is.

Bill begins to laugh again as Frank storms out of the room yelling as he walks down the hallway in the hospital. Patients and staff are starring at him as he yells.

Frank (yelling)

What the Fuck dude, I banged a female Bigfoot! It happened. Frank banged a female Bigfoot! Frank banged a female Bigfoot! I had her stank all over my fingers! Frank banged a female Bigfoot! That's it, I am going back to the Fucking woods to find Bessy! Fuck you Bill, Fuck you Quoteboy. Your President is Orange! I am going back to the Fucking woods!

Bill

Oh that was priceless. I was just Fucking with him. I remember everything.

Quoteboy

Should I "go run" down the hall after him?

Bill

No, let him sweat this one out.

Quoteboy smiles.

Quoteboy

I get it, "this" was humorous.

Bill points at Quoteboy.

Bill

Yes, Exactly.

Quoteboy gets up from his chair smiling.

Quoteboy

I will be right "back I" have to go to the facilities and tinkle.

Quoteboy starts to walk towards the door to exit the room.

Bill

Just use the toilet in this room.

Quoteboy looks back at Bill.

Quoteboy

That bathroom "is teaming" with your bacteria.

Bill

Aren't all bathrooms full of bacteria?

Quoteboy

Most are yes that is a true statement but on the "way in" here I passed the cleaning lady cleaning the facilities by the elevator. I noticed that she used a bleach based cleaner, I should have another fifteen minutes "or so" to use the facilities and still reap the benefits of the bacteria killing Bleach cleaning solution.

Bill

You are Fucking with me right?

Quoteboy

On "the" contrary.

Bill

Let me ask you this. How do you know the cleaning lady wasn't a Democrat?

Quoteboy

She cleaned with Bleach. Good old fashioned don't "get it in your" eyes or it will burn Bleach. She didn't clean it with some Liberal environmentally friendly nondiscriminatory safe "for" all to use cleaner. I will "be using" that bathroom. It has "been recently" cleaned and I prefer clean bathrooms to go tinkles.

Bill shakes his head from side to side.

Bill

And Quoteboy. Look at me. If I ever hear you say you have to tinkle again. I will punch the Fucking Shit out of you. You are a grown ass man. Say you have to take a Fucking Piss. Say it.

Quoteboy

I don't feel the "need to" use those words.

Bill starts to get out of the bed.

Bill

Fucking say it.

Quoteboy

I don't "really" want to.

Bill

Fucking say it.

Quoteboy takes a step back and nervously speaks.

Quoteboy

I am going to go pee.

Bill shakes his head from side to side in disbelief.

Bill

Remind me again why we are friends?

Quoteboy

From the Sixth grade through the Twelfth grade I completed "all of your" homework assignments, class projects and provided you with the majority of "your correct" test answers. In return you beat "the Fuck" out of anyone who picked on me because of my air quotes or conspiracy theories. For which I am forever grateful.

Bill

Look, I still don't get the air quotes and the conspiracy theory Bull Shit can drive me

Fucking nuts but I will still beat the Fuck out of anyone who picks on you.

Quoteboy smiles as applies hand sanitizer to his fingers.

Quoteboy

I know "you" would.

Bill

Hey, tell me your wildest conspiracy theory, the craziest scenario you believe in.

Quoteboy

Why, you "won't" believe me. To air quote Jack Nicholson "in a" Few Good Men. "You can't handle the Truth."

Bill

Try me.

Quoteboy

Bernie Sanders isn't Human.

Bill

Come again?

Quoteboy

Bernie Sanders is "an" animatronic Cyborg created by DICK.

Bill

Dick? Dick who?

Quoteboy

DICK is not a person. It is an "acronym" for the Democratic International Cult Klan which is helmed by Beth Higgens, the last known female "to" have willing intercourse with our friend Frank. Notice how I stated "willing" intercourse.

Bill

You are right. I can't handle the Fucking truth.

Quoteboy turns to walk towards the door.

Bill (continued)

Hey before you go, say it. Fucking say it right.

Quoteboy

I am going to "take a" Fucking Piss like a grown ass Mutha Fuckn' man.

Bill claps.

Bill

There you go. No more saying tinkles. Boys under the age of five go tinkles, not grown ass men.

Quoteboy speaks with confidence and volume.

Quoteboy

I am a grown "ass man" who pisses. I sometimes don't even lift up the toilet seat.

Bill

OK that is a little rude. You should always lift the toilet seat. It is just good manners.

Quoteboy

"Got" it. Can I go now. I don't want to have an accident. Mom "complains about" doing the laundry after I have accidents.

Bill

Hey did you ever find your Jeff Sessions doll?

Quoteboy

I did not. I fear he is "lost and" alone in the vast woods. I did replace him with a Sara Huckabee Sanders doll. She "is" great. If you pull her string she says "There is no collusion."

Bill laughs and points towards the door.

Bill

Don't run into any of Beth Higgen's Hitmen in the Men's room.

Quoteboy exits the room quickly.

CHAPETR TWELVE - DEMOCRATIC HITMEN

Day. Interior. Bathroom.

Quoteboy is standing at the middle urinal holding his penis with both hands as he is going pee when two men enter the bathroom dressed in black suits and sunglasses. One man stands to the urinal on the left and one on the right of Quoteboy. Quoteboy glances over to his left and then to his right. Quoteboy has to let go of his penis so he can make air quotes.

Quoteboy

You gentlemen dressed alike today. Statistically "the odds of" that happening are pretty remote unless you "both" know each other, then "the" odds definitely become tipped in your favor.

The man to the right of Quoteboy begins to speak.

Man in Black #1

We are watching you.

Quoteboy stares at the man speaking.

Quoteboy

You are "what" now?

Man in Black #1

Don't make us send the Elite Democratic Hitmen to your home.

Quoteboy begins to dribble pee onto his pants leg as he nervously replies.

Quoteboy

What? You must "have me confused" with someone else.

The second man in black begins to speak.

Man in Black #2

You live in the basement of your Mother's home at 45 Electric Avenue, Brea California.

You sleep on your childhood bed. Your walls are covered in X-Files and Star Trek posters. You have been openly air quoting since 1999. You refuse to eat Ziti pasta because you feel it is linked somehow to a future zombie apocalypse. You committed voter fraud by voting for Donald Trump 237 times under different aliases. You claim to have slept with eleven women but we both know the real number is one. Shall I continue?

Quoteboy

It's like your "inside" my head.

Man in Black #1 stares at Quoteboy.

Man in Black #1

Stop talking about the Democratic Hitman Squad or they will pay a visit to your home. Are we clear?

Quoteboy quickly puts his penis away and zips up his pants.

Quoteboy

Oh my God you "guys are" real.

Man in Black #2

We were never here.

Quoteboy

You are behind "some" of this Countries darkest secrets. I have to know. Please tell "me is" Bigfoot a Republican or a Democrat? Please, please say Republican.

Man in black #1 looks at man in black number two and nods his head yes.

Man in Black #2

The proof is on Frank's fingers.

Both Men in Black start to exit the bathroom but are stopped by Quoteboy.

Quoteboy

Wait. I don't "understand what" that means. I think that is what Frank "would" call a Bruce Willis line.

The Men in Black turn back to face Quoteboy.

Man in Black #2

Do you really think a Democrat has the ability to produce a Pussy that smells like moldy cheese and old lady clothes?

Quoteboy

It was my understanding that the Democrats "engineered" Bigfoot to become an Elite Assassin.

Man in Black #2 leans in close to Quoteboy and smiles.

Man in Black #2

That is Fake News. I like your dedication to your beliefs so I'm going to throw you a bone. The Republicans engineered Bigfoot not the Democrats. A young Richard Nixon ran the covert Bigfoot Assassin program in 1947 codename Foot Fucker. That's all I am telling you. The rest, you can figure out yourself. The answers can be found with Bessy.

Quoteboy's jaw drops as he covers his mouth with his hands in disbelief.

Quoteboy

No 'that" can't be. Wait, please one more thing. I have to know. Did "Donald" Trump's inauguration have more people in attendance than any other inauguration in history? I need to know.

Man in Black number one turns back towards Quoteboy and laughs.

Man in Black #1

Now that was Fake News.

Quoteboy removes his Make America Great Again hat from his head.

Quoteboy

That was a lie? A real "actual" lie? Not an Alternative Fact Trath but a real lie?

Man in Black #1

Not everything is a conspiracy.

The Men in Black exit the bathroom as Quoteboy calls out to them.

Quoteboy

You didn't wash "your" hands. That could spread bacteria. Hitmen or no "hitmen you" still need to follow bathroom etiquette. I could supply you "with" a vast number of statistics on hand washing.

Quoteboy walks over to the sink and washes his hands and looks into the mirror and speaks to himself out loud.

Quoteboy (continued)

I need to go back to the "woods and" find Bessy. If I find Bessy, I will find the truth. I'll "need" cameras, sonar, inferred detection systems, night vision goggles, a bug out bag and my Sarah Huckabee Sanders doll. The list goes on and on. I need to "go" now. If Art Bell could see me now. This is for you Art. Out of my way Crisis Actors from Central Casting. Quoteboy is going "back to" the woods. Frank, wait "for" me. Wait for Quoteboy Frank. "Wait." Wait. I'll make more Glucose IV bags! Lock her up! "Lock" her up! Lock her up!

Quoteboy quickly exits the bathroom waving his Make America Great Again hat.

CHAPTER THIRTEEN- DRANK THE BONG WATER

Day. Interior. House.

Frank wakes up on his brother Mitch's brown ripped leather couch. He is confused, extremely high and has a headache. There is a huge Bong sitting on the coffee table next to him with a small mound of marijuana next to it. Frank's brother Mitch and his friend Bill are sitting across of Frank playing video games on a 70- inch TV screen.

Frank

Dude I had the most Fucked up dream.

Mitch

Welcome back to the living Bro. You were passed the Fuck out for like 36 hours.

Bill

We thought you were dead Bro. The only reason we knew you weren't, is you kept farting.

Frank rubs his eyes.

Frank

Dude this dream I had was so real.

Mitch

I'm not surprised. You were hitting that Bong pretty damn hard Bro. Smoking up that new Shit I bought off Skinny Pete. He calls it Bigfoot. On account that when you smoke it, you pass out for like two Fucking days and wake up all smelly and unshaven like a Fucking Bigfoot.

Frank stares at Mitch.

Frank

He calls the Pot, Bigfoot?

Bill

Yeh Bro.

Frank

Guys listen this dream. I was on a hike with two guys, one was like a perfect dude with muscles named Bill and the other was this annoying dude named Quoteboy who used air quotes when he talked and drank from IV bags and he was big into conspiracy theories and hand sanitizer. He kept yapping about a Democratic Hitman Squad.

Mitch

That is Fucked up Bro. That's what you get for drinking the Bong water. I told you don't drink that Shit but you just downed it like a damn Vitamin Water.

Frank

I drank the Bong water?

Bill

Every time Bro.

Frank

It gets more nuts. I banged a female Bigfoot named Bessy and I met this Mountain Man named Mitch.

Mitch pauses playing his video game and smiles at Frank.

Mitch

Hey that's my name Bro.

Frank

This Mountain Man Mitch lived in an underground bunker under a hunting cabin in the middle of the Fucking woods. The entire thing was Fucking nuts. And this Bigfoot, her Pussy smelled like moldy cheese and old lady clothes. How Fucked up is that? I got her stank all over my fingers and she stole my Butter stick.

Frank

Sounds Fucked up Bro.

Bill

It was just a really Fucked up dream Bro. It was the Bigfoot weed talking. You smoked like a pound of it Bro.

Frank grabs his head with his hands and lowers his head down towards his chest.

Frank

My head does Fucking hurt. It just seemed so damn real.

Bill

Just a dream Bro. Aint' no such thing as an Elite Squad of Democratic Hitmen from the Dark State.

Mitch drops his video game controller. He glares at Bill with disbelief. Frank raises his head.

Frank

I never said they were an Elite Squad of Democratic Hitmen from the Dark State. All I said was Democratic Hitmen.

Bill appears to get nervous as he opens a beer and drinks it.

Bill

Sure you did Bro.

Frank becomes defensive and sarcastic.

Frank

Nope. I didn't. Bro.

Mitch

Bro. you have been passed out for almost two days smoking grade A Bigfoot out of a Bong. I'm sure your mind is playing tricks on your ass right now. I heard you say Democratic Hitmen from the Dark State too.

Frank rubs his hands on his face and then stands up and walks towards the window.

Frank

Maybe your right. My head feels like it's being Fucked with a Jackhammer.

Bill

It's the Bigfoot weed Bro.

Frank looks out the window and sees two men dressed in all black standing on the sidewalk next to a women wearing a black dress and black sunglasses smoking a cigarette. Frank notices that they see him looking at them. The woman smiles up towards the window as she pulls out her cell phone and then she motions the two men dressed in black to leave. All three enter a black sedan and drive away. Frank catches the license plate it reads B. Higgens.

Mitch

Sit down Bro. It was all just a dream. Smoke some more Bigfoot. It will make you feel better.

Bill

Just a dream Bro. none of it was real.

Mitch resumes playing his video game as Frank walks back towards the couch and hesitantly sits down. He looks at Bill as Bill's cell phone rings. Bill looks at the number, looks back at Frank and then he exits the room. Frank raises his fingers to his face and smells moldy cheese and old lady clothes. Frank's eyes widen as Mitch looks back at Frank as the video game says Game Over on the large 70- inch TV screen.

THE END

Epilogue

There you have it. That is Frank's Bigfoot story. So you can make your own judgement call on whether Frank did indeed Bang a female Bigfoot or was it all just a dream from a Fat Stoner on a lazy Saturday afternoon passed out on a couch or maybe it was part of a vast Government cover-up. I guess the proof will always be on Frank's fingertips.

Stay tuned for the follow up book, that will answer all your lingering questions. **'FRANK BANGED A FEMALE BOGFOOT, AGAIN!'**

Written by

William Martin

Copyright # 6806957511

2018 ©

Marwil6719@yahoo.com

DaddyDrummer Publishing and Productions.

William Martin has many screenplays available for purchase to read and enjoy. Each screenplay comes bound and personally singed. Email for a complete list.
Marwil6719@yahoo.com

Here are the best sellers-

- Ugly Nanny
- Inappropriate
- Driving Upside down
- Archie's Day
- The Harvest
- Jesus or Gin
- Reflections
- Vocatus
- Cocktail Cop
- Circle of Trust
- Bottoms Up
- Mr. Soto

www.ingramcontent.com/pod-product-compliance
Lightning Source LLC
Chambersburg PA
CBHW060425130626
46555CB00005B/2222